Lessons in Love®

Linda Andrade Wheeler, Ed.D.

Published and distributed by
ISLAND HERITAGE PUBLISHING
ISBN 0-89610-179-7

Address orders and correspondence to:

94-411 Kō'aki Street
Waipahu, Hawai'i 96797
Fax 808-564-8888
Telephone 800-468-2800
www.islandheritage.com

Printed in Hong Kong
First edition, Third printing 2005

Photography by
Veronica Carmona

Book Design by
Sachi Kuwahara Goodwin

Dedicated
to the ones I love

Love is just friendship on fire.
To love, you must first learn
how to be a friend.

A friend is someone who accepts and
loves you unconditionally — despite
your frailties, faults, failures and flaws.
Love is that great spiritual fire between
two friends that can keep burning
throughout their lives to bring warmth
and security. However, it is a fire that
must be tended with great care. Do not
let the flame burn out! Consistent
attention and caring must be given to it
so the fire will keep burning.

Be loyal
to those who love you.

You are truly blessed when someone
loves you. A person has picked you
from the masses of people in the world
to love. Regard that love as sacred
and take care of it as you would
a treasure that you have found in life.
Some people go through life not
knowing the magnificence of love
because they failed to see
the value of love itself.

Love is not what you talk about...
It is what you do.

Do not believe people who just *tell* you
they love you — make sure you see it in
how they treat you. Love is a feeling that
must be experienced by your heart. When
you love, love completely with your heart,
soul and body. The essence of your love
will be in what you do for those you love.
People may remember your smile, your
words, your favorite things, even, perhaps,
your mannerisms; however, what they will
not forget, and what will remain in their
hearts, is how you treated them. In love,
your actions will speak louder for you than
any words you can ever utter. The things
you do for love will never be erased from
people's hearts.

I wish to feel the rhythm of my soul, and dance to its music.

Everyone should have the look of one
in love. That is a time when you feel
at your best and act most beautiful
– both inside and outside. It is an
empowering force that illuminates the
body and awakens the human spirit.

**Physical love is the easy part —
loving with your heart
is the hard part.**

Anyone can touch another person's
body. It is an ordinary act done by
ordinary human beings. But it takes
an extraordinary person to touch the
heart and soul of another human being
and light the fire of love between them.

Love is not a game you play
with another's heart.
It is an experience
you give a person for a lifetime.

The human heart is a very fragile organ
that, if broken, can take a lifetime
to mend. Be kind. Tread gently
and honorably. Let your love be
a commitment of spirits to honor each
other in spite of the changes that may
occur along your life's journey.

When you love someone
who cheats —
you lose.

Heartbreaks are just temporary
inconveniences in life. They are like
pit stops for making your life better.
Remember that one who truly loves you
will not make you unhappy. Go find the
person who makes you feel at your best
and will love you for who you are.

Lover's Irony:

How different we are, You and I, so much alike, Together complete.

Love is an amazing phenomenon that has no reason for its spell. It is two human spirits coming together and knowing that together they are one. It is not what is seen that makes their love special; it is what they both feel in their hearts that simply cannot be measured by any human tool.

**Life's long road fades
when hearts together rejoice
each day's joyous moments!**

Love is growing old together —
when two people make each other feel
the glow of their golden years
with curiosity and excitement.
It is the linking of two people's past
and present and the brightness
of their future together.

**Love is beauty you see
with your heart
and not with your eyes.**

Love knows no boundaries
— it is limitless. It leaps cultures,
personalities and disabilities.
When you truly love, you see beyond
what you see. You don't want people to
like you or love you for your wrapping.
You want them to like or love you
for the gift that is inside
— that specialness that will get
better over time and last forever.

With the warmth of
yesterday's breeze still about you,
you come to me in spiritual meeting,
consoling my quivering heart.

Love is not forever.
It may not even be life-lasting; but when
it happens, something magical occurs
between two people that they will never
forget their entire lives, and their lives
will have been changed forever
from that experience.

Entice me, my love,
to life's fullness and pleasures
with you beside me.

Love is the freedom of the soul to
soar beyond earthly boundaries in
partnership and to enter a spiritual
place on earth. It is where peace and
joy can be found at the same time.
In essence, it is truly heaven on earth.

Love has nothing to do with what you are expecting to get, only with what you are expecting to give — which is everything!

Only when you are willing to give
to another person and to have no
expectations as to what is returned
will you reap the benefits of that love.
High expectations bring
deep disappointments.

**Laughter fills the cup
so empty in loneliness.
Come, gush my vessel full!**

Laughter is the music of love.
It is the opening of your soul to find the
joy in another person's experience.
It is often said that grief binds
two people forever. But the picture they
may have of that bond is one of sorrow.
However, when two people are joined
by joy, the image etched in their
togetherness is one of merriment.

It's never too late to love.

Young people may think love is reserved
for them, but it is really for the young at
heart. No matter how old you become,
your heart retains its youthfulness
when you love and are loved in return.

To be happy,
you must risk unhappiness.

Since you are not alone on a deserted
island, you are sometimes influenced by
the opinions of others, which may be in
contrast to your own. When you go
with your heart in matters of love, you
are bound to displease or upset other
people. Listen to your heart.
The unhappiness may be temporary,
but your happiness can be permanent.

When the passion dies within you, love ceases for two people.

Why do people think that when their
passion runs dry for someone, they
create a desert for themselves only?
They do not. The death of passion in a
love affair is the burial of two hearts
that were once inflamed with love.

**Yesterday's hurt
is today's understanding
rewoven into tomorrow's love.**

You gain a deeper insight into the
value of love when you have
experienced the painful truths of love.
Love is something you give another
person. But it does not always mean
that the other person receives it to the
same degree you have given it.
Remember that you are the
worthy person for having given it.
Do not be ashamed of it.

Never get attached to someone who does not love you back.

When someone tells you they do not
love you, accept that. Do not try
to make them love you – it will not
work. Let go of the person.
Set them free and on their own path.
Love takes caring and attention, and
that takes lots of positive energy.
Spend your precious moments and
valuable time on people who love and
care about you. You will be surprised at
the returns of that kind of special love.

Love the person, not the things that
come with the person.
Otherwise, when the things fade,
so will the person.

In love, do not ask of the other person
what you yourself cannot give.
Give and ask only what you can and
are willing to give to another yourself.
By doing this, you show the person you
love that you are fair and honest.

In love, not getting what you want is sometimes a stroke of luck.

God in His goodness orchestrates life to help you see the clarity and truth in who you are and what you can become. Sometimes when you are in love, it is difficult to understand when things do not work out the way you planned. But as time goes by, things reveal themselves clearly and you know you made a wise decision — your life could have been drastically altered if you had gotten what you initially wanted.

**You know you are a success
if your children love you.**

The enormous love parents have for
their children can only be felt in their
actions to them throughout their lives.
Children's love for their parents is God's
ultimate gift to parents, and it comes
about because the precious heavenly
gifts He gave them were highly-valued
and well-cared for on earth.

When you lose in love,
don't lose the lesson.

Everything in life teaches you something,
whether it is a happy or painful experience.
Learning the lessons of life depends
upon how much you want to learn.
Successes, like failures, are experiences
that help you appreciate your investment
in yourself and in others' lives.

Mending yourself from a broken
heart is something you do alone,
in your own way, in your own time.

When you are heartbroken, take time to
feel all the emotions that are making
you feel sad. Cry if you must.
Crying is the cleansing of the soul.
And when you are done, look at all the
wonderful things you have in life that
another person cannot give you or
money cannot buy. It is then that you
will realize you are lucky to be alive.
Find a friend who cares about you and
can laugh with you. Laughter is the
healing of the heart. Laugh a lot!

You forgive
to the extent that you love.

People who love know it is a valuable
commodity and cannot be wasted. They
also know that forgiving cannot change
the past, but it can enlarge their future.
You keep people you love in your life
when you forgive the things they do.

Love is a choice you make for yourself.

No one can make the perfect match
of hearts except the people who make
the commitment to love one another.
Each person magically finds the half
of their soul in someone else's heart.
Two people become one when their
souls speak to each other and know
that together their hearts beat as one.

**It is when you give of yourself
that you truly give to others.**

People who know how special they are
and share that uniqueness with others
every day make life exciting and different
each day. Unique people are the great
"chefs" of life who create a varied and
exciting life menu. They know that
being themselves, they bring diversity
— the main ingredient in spicing up life.

To love oneself is the beginning
of a lifelong romance.

Love yourself as if you were your most
treasured lover. Then and only then
can you measure the extent that you can
love another completely.

**Especially with loved ones,
remember that nothing lasts forever.
Live each day as if it were
your last day with them.**

How easy it is to forget the value of time
spent with those you love. In the
routine of everyday responsibilities,
you may not once stop to think that
those moments may never occur again.
Remind yourself to look around you
and be grateful for the present
moments you have with loved ones.
They come just once in a lifetime.
Treasure them.

If you want to be loved, you must love.

You might say to one who loves you,
"I love you because you love me."
However, when you stop loving
someone, you cannot expect the other
person to continue loving you. You
must give love in order to get love.

Words are the voice of the heart;
eyes are the window to the soul.

Whenever you speak of love, make sure
you have the full attention of the one
you are sharing your heart with, for it is
through the eyes of your lover that you
will see the person's heart and feel
the intensity of love for you.

Everybody is somebody special.
Treat everyone with that in mind.

You know you are different from others.
That should tell you something.
That perspective of how special you
are will help you acknowledge and
appreciate the uniqueness of others.
Welcome and celebrate their differences
to live life in an exciting and special way.

**People like you to the extent
that they feel comfortable
in your presence.**

It is so wonderful to be in the company
of people who accept and appreciate
you for who you are. They have no
pretenses as to who they are, and
they simply expect you to be you.
When someone tells you they like you,
honor and celebrate that
— it is the bud of love.

**The love in your heart
was not put there to stay.
Love is not love
until it is given away.**

Why do people keep in their hearts
words they should express to another
they adore? If spoken, their feelings can
touch another's heart to bring love to
their own. Love is the greatest emotion
any human being can feel. You deny
yourself that great experience
when you hide your love.

**When you make a commitment,
you must do everything you can
to keep it.**

Many times, the only thing you have
is your good word. You can use that to
build trust in your relationships and
a good reputation to maintain them.
You will gain the loyalty and love of
those whom you are consistent
with in your behaviors.

Nothing binds us one to the other
like a promise kept. Nothing divides us
like a promise broken.
People who keep their promises,
help others to keep theirs.

Nothing in life is guaranteed.
That is a given. But people have great
personal power to control the things
they do in life. Those who know how to
control their power and fulfill promises
are blessed with people who trust and
honor them. Those who break promises
as if they were little twigs off a rotten
tree flounder their whole lives,
spreading seeds on barren ground.

**Treat others the way
you want to be treated,
only do it first.**

My mom once said, "Make friends even
if you don't need them." I never forgot
that because it laid the foundation of my
relationships. It brought focus to the
meaning of friendship, and how one
should treat others. By simply doing the
right things to and for people,
you show them how people like to
be treated and valued.

Sometimes in love,
experience can be harmful.
It can prevent you from trying again.

How unfortunate it is when you
experience a love affair filled with pain,
deception and mistrust. It is those times
that one must have the courage to look
at that lesson, learn from it,
and go on to better experiences.

Tune in to people.
Give them what they need so they
can feel good about themselves.

People are like flowers. You've got to
know what kind of flowers they are to
give them the kind of attention and
nourishment they need. Someone like
a daisy needs constant attention and
watering, whereas a cactus would die
from that same treatment. Bring
balance to your life with different kinds
of flowers — they will challenge you
and make your life more exciting.

Make people feel welcomed, needed and appreciated. The greatest hunger people have is to be needed, wanted and loved.

Everyone wants to be included in life
with people they like and love.
You can make them feel part of your life
by listening to them, sharing your
experiences with them and spending
time with them.

**Love yourself.
If you become like someone else,
you will always be number 2.**

Your uniqueness is a gift you share with
others. It is your influencing statement
in life — the personal impression you
leave with others. There is no one like
you in the whole world. Know that
everyone you meet will have their own
gifts to share. Let them be proud of
their offerings, give each person the
opportunity to be their best self, and
you will enjoy the specialness of everyone.

Be kind — it's powerful!

Kindness can be shown in a variety
of ways. One way is to compliment
at least three people a day — you will
make them feel good, and, in the
process, lift your own spirits. Do it
consistently, and you will help those
around you learn this powerful and
positive human force. It is contagious.

**Be happy — think of all the things
you don't get that you don't want.**

When you are envious or jealous about
another's good fortune, look into your
own life and honestly assess all the
things you don't get — illness, bondage,
abuse, etc. It is life's way of being kind
to you; be grateful for your blessings.

Ask yourself, "Am I a joy to live with everyday?"

Naturally, this is a question that on the
surface you would probably answer,
"Of course." But on closer examination,
you may begin to realize all the
unique "stuff" you find in yourself
that may irritate another person.
However, wouldn't you like to be a joy
to live with everyday? Perhaps the
word "joy" gives you the best advice:
Just Offer You.

Love is not
a competitive sport.

Don't compare your love to another
person's brand of love. It is simply not
the same. Your needs, your desires and
the hopes you have packaged for life are
oftentimes very different from those you
want to compare your life with.

Absence makes the heart grow fonder
— unless you cannot believe in your
heart what you do not see.

Loyalty in love stems from the heart
and not from the eyes. If you truly love
another, you have that person etched in
your heart wherever you go. You crave
the person you love when you are apart.
Be true to your heart.

In lost love, if you pursue revenge, you should dig two graves.

Do not use revenge to get back at
someone who has disappointed you in
love. It will be a lose-lose proposition.
Forget the person, pick up your crushed
heart and get a fresh attitude. Take
a new path in life, one you can control
and feel good about. Along the way,
you may just meet someone especially
for you, who is worthy of your love.

Criticism never improves love.

In whatever form it is dished out,
criticism does no good. It does not
elevate your self-esteem or your
goodwill. People do not perform
at their best with criticism.

All people can feel kindness
— it is not only conveyed in words, but
in actions that make people feel cared
for and respected for who they are.

Kindness — the ability to be considerate
and kind to others on a consistent basis
— is one of life's most valuable gifts.
People who are kind naturally see
themselves as peacemakers. They view
the world and everything in it as part
of themselves, so they are careful and
mindful that they play a big part in
what happens to them and to the
people in their lives.

**No one is guaranteed happiness.
It is something you bring to yourself.**

It would be nice to have our birth
certificates stamped with the words
"Happiness Guaranteed." But it would
mean we would not have to take
responsibility for anything that
happened to us. What purpose and
meaning could we find in a life like that?
In this world, people who are happy
work hard to be happy. Happiness is
not something they automatically get
for doing nothing. It is a gift they get in
return for giving themselves to others.

A smile is the emotional sunshine you give another — and what you get in return may change your life.

Many a romantic relationship has started with a smile. It is the universal language of kindness. And when you show you are kind, it is like kindling a spark that may come to flame. A smile may very well ignite the fire of love. Have you ever seen a smiling face that was not beautiful?

**Love is designed
to make you better,
not bitter.**

When you are bitter about something or
someone, you waste precious moments
of life and positive energy focusing on
that. Instead, look at the more positive
things about life and learn from your
disappointments to make you a better
person. It will enlarge your future.

An optimist looks at love like a
flower on a plant in bloom;
a pessimist can't even see the flower.

When you are optimistic about life,
everything in it seems to have a place
and a reason for being, no matter what
form of life it takes. The beauty of life
and people is not always seen through
the eyes. Deeper beauty is in the mind
and spirit of a person. Optimists are more
likely to capture the beauty of a person or
thing because their attitudes are positive
and their hearts are open to newness.

**Saddened hearts awake
to life's harsh realities,
faintly understood.**

Are there really victims in love affairs,
or are they just willing volunteers at the
mercy of someone else's poor conduct
and uncaring heart? In love, it is not
always clear whom you are giving your
heart to, so you must accept the
unknowing as part of the experience.
Once you know someone is not worthy
of your love, do not be caught in the
web of deception. Sometimes a rude
awakening to some painful truth brings
clarity where there was none.

Parents give life
and teach love to their children.

Parents can teach so much

to their children about love.

All they have to do is to love each other.

It is a perpetual lesson that is

indelible in children's minds.

**When a womanizer
marries his mistress,
it leaves a vacancy for another.**

Womanizers are unhappy men who seek
happiness, yet can never be happy
because where they are hunting is void
of it. They must first look into their
hearts, and know what it means to love
themselves first before they can feel
worthy to love another completely.

When you're over the hill, you pick up speed.

It is when you are going up the hill that life challenges you and teaches you valuable lessons. If you learn this well, when you are over the hill, you pick up the speed to value each day and fill your precious moments with people, things and events that make you happy.

**Love is the fire of life; it can either
purify you or consume you.
You determine which.**

When love dazzles you with the passion
and fire of your lover, you become
oblivious to all those around you – you
are in a state of existence that cuts you
off from the realities of life. On the
other hand, love that makes you a better
person to your lover and those around
you brings purpose and meaning to life,
thereby embracing the realities of life.

The cages we build when we clip
each other's wings!
Who are we to tamper
with God's creations?

To love others on a deep and sincere
level, let them be who they are.
They have gifts no other can bring you
and gifts you may not have yourself.
They bring that to share with you, the one
they trust will take care of their heart.
Let them be whole in your presence.

**Love goes to those
who are worthy of it
— not to those who lay in wait for it,
or ignore it when it falls in their laps.**

When love comes your way —
seize it with both hands.
Know in your heart what you want
and act upon it, even though it may
change your life completely.
Because if you don't, your life will be
completely changed forever.

**You show who you are
by those you love.**

When you choose a lover, it is not
simply loving that one person.
It is communicating to others
who you are, what your values are in
life, what you want out of life
and what you hope to become.

**Be kind to yourself.
The emotion you bring to a situation
is what people will feel.**

Who you are, what you think and how
you behave determines the reaction you
will get from others. Every relationship
you build or destroy is your own.
Think of yourself as a builder and
you will build.

**There is no me
without you.**

Know who does or does not matter.
When you care about a person,
everything about the person matters.
When you don't care, nothing matters
about the person. When you discover
who makes life better than being alone,
then your life will be complete, and you
will not want to be alone.

There is only one corner of the
universe you can be certain of
improving, and that is your own self.

Things do not change. We change.
If you change yourself to build the kind
of relationships you want, the lifestyle
you desire and the future you envision
for yourself, then you are more likely to
reach your goals faster than if you wait
around for others to change. Change is
a personal matter. Make it happen and
be sure to make it work for you.

Be the best wherever you are and with whomever you are at the time.

You craft the version of your best or worst self. Nobody does that for you. Excellence is an inside job that takes effort and consistent attention. When you are at your best, you feel good — physically, emotionally, intellectually, spiritually and socially. You are in sync with the universe and everything in it. Do everything possible — develop a positive attitude, acquire the necessary knowledge and sharpen your skills — to be at your best so you can feel good and share that with others.

Knowing that only God is in
a position to look down on others,
it is better to look people in
the eye and think well of them.

No one gets out of this world without
experiencing a put-down from someone.
Why do people think they are better
than anyone else?
Perhaps they have not taken the time
to know others and the tremendous
gifts they have that others cannot see.
Even a diamond does not reveal its
sparkle to everyone; only those who
believe there is something in the stone
will work hard to see its inner beauty.

You get from life what you are willing to put in it.

Life is wonderful.
Everything you need to make you happy
is already in life. It is what you are
willing to invest in life — the time you
spend to show people you love them,
the things that you do for others, how
you use your gifts and strengths — that
will produce either the fruits of your
labor or the emptiness of what you
failed to put into life.

**Feel into your heart
so you can feel mine.**

In love, your heart will dictate your
actions toward others to show how
much you care about them. Fill your
heart with love so others can feel it, too.
Help them see it clearly by doing things
for them that they translate as love.

The heart so peaceful once —
no steady beat remains.

Love is a rejuvenating experience. It
makes you feel younger, more beautiful
and less vulnerable to pain. Life takes on
a rhythmic and peaceful beat when you
feel secure in love. Yet, when love stops,
the reverse happens. You feel hopelessly
helpless, alone, unattractive and some-
how older. It is at these times that you
must look at love as an experience that
changes you, perhaps not physically, but
in more important ways than that — in
your mind — and remind yourself that the
experience of love is a growing process,
and that you are still alive. Know that like
the stars that come out every night, the
rhythm of life will come back again.

**Encompassing soul,
forbidding entry or exit,
creates love's blockade.**

Love comes to all who let it happen.
It is a personal experience that is
controlled only by you — you either
respond to love or you reject it. That is
a choice only you can make. When you
close your mind and heart to love, you
miss out on the wonderful experience of
being human — to feel the heights of
your soul, and to be able to fly in the
company of a person who loves you.

They say if you understand yourself,
you understand all people.
However, when you love someone,
you learn something about yourself.

It is one thing to touch one's mind — it is
an activity of logic. Reason is securely
lodged within the brain and body of the
person. When you touch another
person's heart, it is an activity of the
soul. It leaves the body and meets
another soul to communicate on a level
that only two people can understand.
To convey the feelings of love to another
is the highest level of communication
between two human beings. It is then
that you discover the power within you
that makes another person's heart tick.

When your tendency is to blame
another person for how you feel,
look in the mirror and remind
yourself that who you see is the only
person responsible for your happiness.

It is so empowering to realize that your
life can be controlled by you – and you
alone. Never give that power away to
someone else who may be careless in
using it. You determine what makes you
happy. Your happiness is the result of
the responsibility you take everyday in
your life to make it happen.

Created Bond

**Unspoken splendor of friendship,
reflected in genuine acts of loving
kindnesses, pierces souls eternally.**

A friend is a treasure you find for
yourself. You instinctively know the
worth of a friend in the way you are
treated and valued when you are alone
and in the company of others. How is a
friendship measured? By the lasting
effect it has on your life.

**Encaged within,
my heart sings out — Let me fly
in the shadow of your span.**

When you are unable to be with the one
you love, you simply want to be near
the person — to be able to see, hear or
maybe touch the person. It is one of
life's harsh realities that sometimes no
matter how much you love a person,
you cannot be with that person.

A heart retouched
— blooms again!

Love never dies within you.
It may lay dormant for a period of time;
but it is awakened when another human
being — as if with a magical wand
— touches your spirit and brings it to life
again. It is the rebirth of life within you
— the hopeful spark that lives within
each of us, waiting for the right person
to bring it to eternal flame.